PAIR-IT BOOKS™

CLAP Your Hands!

Written by Katherine Mead

STECK-VAUGHN
ELEMENTARY · SECONDARY · ADULT · LIBRARY

A Harcourt Classroom Education Company

www.steck-vaughn.com

Snap your fingers.

2

Clap your hands.

3

Pat your knees.

 4

Stomp your feet.

Twist your hips.

6

Raise your arms.

Dance!